A NORTH-SOUTH PAPERBACK

Critical praise for

Melinda and Nock
and the Magic Spell

"An underwater fantasy adventure about a young mermaid named Melinda and her water-sprite friend Nock. . . . The watercolor cartoons take readers into this colorful marine world. . . . This humorous offering will appeal."

School Library Journal

"This is a charming little fantasy for beginning readers ready for little chapter books. . . . A fun story . . . with charming illustrations."

Baltimore's Child

Ingrid Uebe

Melinda and Nock
and the Magic Spell

Illustrated by Alex de Wolf

Translated by J. Alison James

North-South Books

NEW YORK / LONDON

First published in the United States, Great Britain, Canada,
Australia, and New Zealand in 1996 by North-South Books,
an imprint of Nord-Süd Verlag AG, Gossau Zürich, Switzerland.
First paperback edition published in 1998 by North-South Books.

Library of Congress Cataloging-in-Publication Data
Uebe, Ingrid.
[Melinda und der Zauber der Meerhexe. English]
Melinda and Nock and the magic spell / Ingrid Uebe ;
illustrated by Alex de Wolf ; translated by J. Alison James.
Summary: When an evil witch's spell changes a mischievous water sprite
into a sea horse, Melinda the mermaid must search the seven seas
for a special pearl that will allow her best friend to return to his true form.
[1. Fairy tales. 2. Mermaids—Fiction.] I. James, J. Alison.
II. Wolf, Alex de, ill. III. Title.
PZ8.U33Me 1996 [Fic]—dc20 95-52218

A CIP catalogue record for this book is available from The British Library.

ISBN 1-55858-571-0 (TRADE BINDING)
1 3 5 7 9 TB 10 8 6 4 2
ISBN 1-55858-572-9 (LIBRARY BINDING)
1 3 5 7 9 LB 10 8 6 4 2
ISBN 1-55858-992-9 (PAPERBACK)
1 3 5 7 9 PB 10 8 6 4 2

Printed in Belgium

For more information about our books, and the authors and artists
who create them, visit our web site: http://www.northsouth.com

CHAPTER ONE

Once upon a time there was a mermaid
named Melinda. She lived with her family
under the sea. Melinda didn't have many
mermaid friends. Of course, there were lots of
other mermaids, but all they ever wanted to do
was sit and comb their hair and sing sad songs.
Melinda was different.

Melinda liked to play among the mussels and the coral. She liked to swim and spin and sing silly songs. Her best friend was Nock, the old water sprite's youngest son. Nock was lively and full of tricks. He had two strong legs like a human, hair as spiky as a sea urchin, and a long, pointy nose just like his father's.

Nock couldn't swim as well as Melinda, but he could ride on a dolphin. He could do water acrobatics. He could dive down to where the sunken ships were, and he always found the best hiding places.

Playing with Nock was always an adventure.

One day Nock said, "I know what would be fun. We can tease the witch."

"Someday, Nock," said Melinda, "you're going to get yourself in trouble."

CHAPTER TWO

Melinda and Nock dived down through a deep crack in the ocean floor to where the water was as dark as squid ink. There they found the witch's cave.

The witch was forever casting spells to get what she wanted. And what she wanted most were jewels. She had a sharp coral fence around her cave and a guard fish to protect her from thieves. She didn't like strangers.

Melinda and Nock glided past the mouth of the cave, along the spiky coral fence. Inside the cave they could see lights: gold and silver, ruby red, emerald green, sapphire blue. And a milky glowing light, like the moon in water.

"It's the jewels," said Nock. "She likes the pearls best."

Melinda knew that whenever a ship sank, the witch was the first on the scene. She covered the area with webs of spells until she was able to get all the treasure for herself.

Melinda and Nock were so quiet, the guard fish didn't notice them as they slipped up and over the sharp fence and swam near the mouth of the cave.

Melinda and Nock hid in a cleft in the rock.
Nock said, "Listen to this, Melinda." Then
he called out in a teasing voice:
  "Mirror, mirror on the wall,
  Who's the ugliest one of all?

It's the witch, of course!
The ugly old witch!"
The witch burst from her cave like a
tidal wave.

She hissed and spat with rage.

Melinda fled to the other side of the fence. But Nock wasn't so lucky. He got caught on a coral.

The witch pounced, and grabbed him by the neck.

She pricked him with her magic wand,
and suddenly Nock was gone. The witch had
turned him into a sea horse!

CHAPTER 3

Melinda was stunned. She was terrified of the witch, but she had to do something. She swam back over the fence and shouted, "Witch, what have you done?"

"He called me ugly!" said the witch, outraged.

"But Nock didn't mean it. He was just fooling around."

"Rudeness must be punished. He will be a sea horse for the rest of his life."

"It was just a game!" Melinda cried. "Now I won't have a best friend to play with."

"Then perhaps you'd like to be a sea horse too," said the witch. "Now go away before I lose my temper."

Melinda grabbed the witch's dress and wailed: "Give me back my friend! I want him back now! I'll do anything you ask, if you only turn him back!"

"Anything at all?" the witch asked.

Melinda nodded nervously.

"All right then," said the witch. "Bring me the Seventh Wonder of the Sea—the most beautiful pearl in the world."

"But where can I find it?" asked Melinda.

"In one of the seven seas, of course."

That meant it could be anywhere in the world.

"How will I know what it looks like?"

The witch laughed. "It is round as a bubble and shines as brightly as the moon, with all the shades of the rainbow."

Melinda made a rope of seaweed, tied it
to Nock, and led him away from the witch's
dark cave.

CHAPTER 4

Melinda swam through the seven seas.
The sea horse always swam behind her. From
time to time she stopped and tried to play
with him, but he just looked at her sadly.
So she swam on.

She searched in every ocean in the world,
but she couldn't find the Seventh Wonder
of the Sea.

She asked the fish.

She asked the octopus and the electric eel.
But none of them had ever seen it.

"Though I'm sure I'd recognize it right away
if I did," said the octopus. "It's supposed to be
the most beautiful jewel in the world."

Sometimes, when land was in sight, Melinda would surface and swim as close as possible to the shore. She asked crabs and birds and polar bears. But the answer was always the same.

She even asked the moon, whose silver light shone down to the bottom of the sea. But the moon didn't answer.

"Oh, Nock," said Melinda. "What are we going to do? If we don't find the pearl, you'll be a sea horse forever."

The sea horse shook his head. He couldn't talk, but he tugged on the line.

"Do you want to go home?" asked Melinda.

The sea horse nodded.

"But I don't know the way anymore," said Melinda miserably. "I'm completely lost!"

Nock tugged on the line again.

"Do you know where to go?" Melinda asked, surprised.

The little sea horse started to swim, and Melinda followed.

CHAPTER FIVE

Melinda and Nock swam for three days and three nights without stopping. They were exhausted when they arrived at Nock's home.

The old water sprite came out. "Melinda!" he cried, and kissed her. He waved the sea horse away. "Shoo! Shoo! Stop pestering Melinda!"

But Melinda cried, "That's not a sea horse! That's Nock!"

Melinda explained what had happened.

The old water sprite laughed. "That sounds like something he'd do. Hey, little Nicker Nocker, is that you?" He tickled the sea horse under the chin. The sea horse knocked away his father's fingers. "That's him all right," said the old sea sprite, laughing again.

"How can you laugh?" asked Melinda.

"I can't believe you went all around the world just to find the Seventh Wonder of the Sea," he said, "when it is right outside the witch's door."

"What!" said Melinda. Nock's sea horse spines stood on end.

"Oh, her guard fish swallowed it years ago. But he'd probably trade it for a dollop of jam."

"Where could we find any jam under the sea?" asked Melinda.

"In my larder, of course," said the old sprite. "I made it just last season from the sea-cherry tree. Little Nocky here pitted the cherries for me. Here, have a jar."

CHAPTER 6

It was getting dark when they arrived at the witch's cave. The guard fish raised his spines when he saw them. "Halt! Who goes there?" he called. "Friend or foe?"

"Friends," called Melinda softly. "We came with a present."

"Hold on, I'll get the witch," said the fish.

"No, wait," said Melinda. "This present isn't for her. It's for you."

"But nobody ever brings me presents."

"It's jam," Melinda said, holding out a spoonful. "Sea-cherry jam."

The guard fish looked tenderly at the mermaid. "I love sea-cherry jam," he said.

The fish opened his mouth and let Melinda dribble in a large spoonful of jam.

Scarcely had he swallowed when *pa-tooie*,
out shot the Seventh Wonder of the Sea.

"Here," said the fish. "You can have this. It's
been hurting my belly anyway. Thanks for the
jam." He looked longingly at the jar.

"Gosh, thanks!" cried Melinda. "Here, have another spoonful."

The sea horse spun for joy.

The pearl shimmered as brightly as the moon, with all the shades of the rainbow. Melinda held it tightly.

Then she called the witch.

CHAPTER SEVEN

Melinda had to call three times before the
witch poked her head out of her door. "Here,"
said Melinda. "I have the Seventh Wonder of
the Sea. If you give me back my friend, I'll give
you the pearl."

With a swift poke of her magic wand,
the witch turned the sea horse back into
little Nock.

He was all there: spiky hair, pointy nose, and bouncy legs. Melinda laughed happily. She handed the witch the pearl and turned to go.

But the witch wasn't finished with them yet. "What is in there?" she asked, pointing to the little glass jar.

"Sea-cherry jam," said Melinda.

"Mmm," said the witch. "I want that, too."

"You can't have it all," said Melinda, "since you've been so awful. But I'll give you a spoonful."

All three of them went into her cave, and Melinda carefully dropped a spoonful of jam into the witch's porridge. The witch laid the Seventh Wonder of the Sea in a special box and went to the fire to warm her porridge. While the witch was busy stirring, Nock led Melinda quietly out of the cave.

Hand in hand the two friends swam up through the crack to their own familiar ocean floor. There they stopped to rest on a rusty chain.

"I am so glad you're not a sea horse anymore," said Melinda. "You were still nice, but I like you better when you can talk!"

"And when I can play tricks again, right?"
Nock asked, grinning. Then he pulled out the
witch's Seventh Wonder of the Sea.

Melinda was astonished. "Did you take it
from her cave?"

"Yes," said Nock. "I switched it with my cherry stone, the one from the sea-cherry tree."

They both had to laugh.

Nock handed Melinda the pearl. "Here," he said. "I got it for you. Thanks for saving my life."

Melinda was delighted, but then she said, "You know, I'm going to take this back to the witch."

"Why?" asked Nock. He looked disappointed.

"I'd really rather have your cherry stone," said Melinda. "I can thread it on a string of seaweed and wear it like a necklace. This pearl is much too large."

Nock laughed, and once again they dived deep down into the crack in the ocean floor.

About the Author

Ingrid Uebe was born in Essen, Germany. She showed an early interest in newspapers, and was the cultural editor of a large daily paper until the birth of her daughter. Since 1977, she has published more than fifty children's books. Ingrid Uebe lives in Cologne, Germany, with the river Rhine running in front of her door, and a pond back in the garden. She loves the sea and goes there as often as she can. She hopes that one day Melinda and little Nock will come close to shore.

About the Illustrator

Alex de Wolf was born in a suburb of Amsterdam. He studied at art school, and because he liked drawing children and animals, he often sat for hours sketching at the zoo. Alex de Wolf lives with his wife and two young sons in Amsterdam. They have a garden outside the city, with a bamboo grove and a pond. There they have regular visits from frogs, rabbits, and hedgehogs. Perhaps one day the witch will come for tea. They will be sure to have some cherry jam on hand.

About the Translator

J. Alison James was born in California and makes her permanent home in Vermont. Recently she spent a year in Japan, and is now living in Norway. Alison James studied languages and got a master's degree in Children's Literature so that she could write and translate books. She has written two novels, and translated over thirty books for North-South. Her first original picture book, *Eucalyptus Wings*, was recently published.

Although Alison James has seen many more than seven wonders in this world, she thinks that the best things are found outside her own back door.